CW00865671

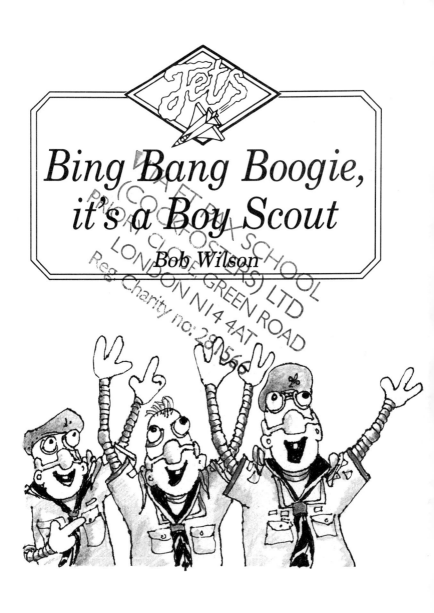

Bing Bang Boogie, it's a Boy Scout

Bob Wilson

A & C Black · London

For Matilda, Reuben and Babik

First published 1997 by A & C Black (Publishers) Ltd
35 Bedford Row, London WC1R 4JH

Copyright © 1997 Bob Wilson
ISBN 0–7136–4652–7

A CIP catalogue record for this book
is available from the British Library.

Filmset by Kalligraphic Design Ltd, Horley, Surrey ·
Printed in Great Britain by William Clowes Ltd, Beccles, Suffolk

Way out in space millions of
billions of squillions of
miles away from the small planet
we call Earth, there is an even
smaller planet called GROB.
On this planet live a race of alien
space monsters called –

THE GROBBLEWOCKIANS.

Once upon a time, back in the 1980s
the Grobblewockians
were said
to be

The Most Evil
CREAT-YORZ
IN DER
YOONY-VERSE!

But not
any more.

3

Things are different now.

Nowadays Grobblewockians have a reputation for being honest, peaceful, law-abiding citizens who spend most of their time thinking of others – and making up names for knots.

Indeed, it's now often said that the average Grobblewockian is so timid *he wouldn't even say 'Boo!' to a goose.*

What brought about this change?

Historians of the future might claim:

That saintly beings of high spiritual intelligence taught the Grobblewockians the error of their ways.

Or maybe historians might claim:

B That the Grobblewockians were put in the care of well-meaning, but power-crazed, dictators who taught them about truth, justice, the dire consequences of anti-social behaviour, and how an oxbow lake is formed.

TeE-CHER
iz a
BiGG
NiT!

...the whole class will stay in at playtime, **and** do extra Geography homework for the rest of term!

But the historians will be wrong.

Because the truth is:

C They gave up being evil because they discovered that...

1. Conquering planets
2. Destroying civilisations
3. Pillaging
4. Looting
5. Murdering innocent bystanders and
6. Vandalising bus shelters

was not half as much fun as

being in ➡️ THE GROBBLEWO

Well, what happened was this...
In 1988 a Grobblewockian called GROTT
came down to Earth in a Scout Ship
and landed in the middle of a Boy Scout Camp.
He wasn't a particularly evil alien – but he
did have a Mega Powerful Laser Ray-Gun
and would have blown the
head off this particular
Boy Scout. But ...

...but that's
another story.

No, I mean it really is another story.
It's a 'JETS' story called...
"Ging Gong Goolie, It's an Alien"
Now this particular Boy Scout's
name was ➡ GARRY WIMBUSH

It was Garry Wimbush
who taught Grott about
Scouting, and how to
speak English – and
you need to know this
because...

he's in this story too.

But this story takes place 64 years later.
The Year is 2052.

AND NOW ➡

THIS IS GARRY WIMBUSH.

He is a grandad.

And, along with the rest of the old 3rd Balsawood Road Scout troop he lives in . . .

A residential establishment providing enablement, sustenance and solace to chronologically deprived ex-members of the outdoor cultural & recreational pursuits movement.

In other words

An Old Folks Home FOR OLD TIME SCOUTS

Some of the old scouts were now short-sighted.

Some were hard of hearing.

And Skip (who was 92), had lost his sense of direction.

But their hearts were strong,
their minds were clear,
and their memories stretched right
back to the good old days.

He was a million, billion, squillion
miles away, on the planet GROB. And
he too was talking about the past.

Grott was very proud
of his grandson.
For Gribble was
a good scout,
and had
earned . . .

Lots of
BAJIZ.

There was however, one badge he
didn't have, one test that he had
failed to pass.
It was:

THE GROBBLEWOCKIAN
BACKWOODSMAN
BADGE

But a good Scout never gives up.
And so today, armed not only with a
fearless spirit – but also with his
grandad's precious picture, he set
out with his troop to try again.

HI-HO! HI-HO
IT'S ♪ TO THE
WOODS WE GO

Grandad Wimbush had a grandson too. His name was . . .

DIMBERT

Today Dimbert was going to visit his grandad. His mother said it might do him some good.

But I'm not interested in scouting.

Well talk about something you <u>are</u> interested in

said his mother.

So he did.

He talked about why he needed a modem upgrade, the disadvantages of RAM doubling on a PC 6500 – and how Squark 7.5B wasn't compatible with an IBM running at 1280Mhz. Then he said:

Grandad Wimbush listened to all this very carefully, thought about it for a moment – and then said:

Now when I tell you that only that morning Dimbert had . . .

Piloted a Venusian space-cruiser through a storm of deadly meteorites.

Fought his way out of an AWESOME monster-infested MAZE-DUNGEON.

Driven a Formula 1 racing car around a GRAND PRIX circuit at 157 miles per hour.

Designed, and virtually constructed a small industrial city.

Played chess with his Web-mate in AUSTRALIA.

And then played Megaball, Hypercop, and Super-Mega-hyper BLAST-O-CRICKET, (amassing a total score of 17,568 not out).

. . . you might wonder what he was so fed up about. And like Grandad Wimbush, you might wonder what he was talking about.

19

'He's talking about computers,' said the tea lady. 'It's computer talk.' Grandad didn't understand computer talk. He thought:

That a **PC** was somebody who went around arresting burglars.

That **RAM** was a male sheep.

That **Software** was what you went to bed in.

That a **Cursor** was someone who swore a lot.

And that **Dot Matrix** was the name of the tea lady.

The name of the tea lady was <u>not</u> Dot Matrix, but she did have a son who was into computers, and so she was able to translate.

He says he's bored.

exclaimed Grandad Wimbush.

A NOTE FROM THE AUTHOR.

You may think it odd that Dimbert knew nothing about CONKERS. But you must remember that this story is set in THE FUTURE. And in 2052 Conkers will be just one of the things that children won't know about any more.

They will also not know about:

skateboards

swings

kites

Catapults

Frisbees

Yo-Yos

buckets and spades

Sledges

Skipping ropes or marbles.

So what **will** they know about?

Computers.

Dimbert loved his computer.

... on the planet GROB,
Gribble and the Grobblewockian
Scouts had a much bigger problem.
They had failed the badge yet again.

We were stumped Grandad. Absolutely stumped.

Now, to earn the Backwoodsman badge you need to have: determination, stamina, fortitude, know-how, resourcefulness and pluck.

You also need to have ... **a wood.**

And that was the problem; GROB was a totally treeless planet.

Gribble and his troop had hiked the length and breadth of it but all they had ever found were ...

stumps!

According to Grandad Grott, there had once been lots of trees. But *Orrice Dee-orrible*, the most evil of all the 'old-style' Grobblewockians, had blasted them all to smithereens while testing his terrible invention.

'What shall we do?' asked Gribble.

Meanwhile...

On a funny little planet called Earth, Dimbert was waiting for a train. He was going home on the **C**omputer-**R**egulated, **A**uto-**I**ntelligent, **Z**one-**I**ntegrated **T**rain **S**ystem – known for short as:

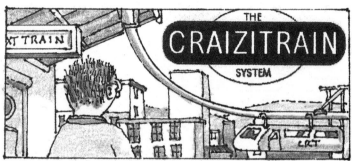

These trains had no driver; they were entirely computer controlled. At first people had worried about this. But scientific experts had assured them.

All the safety systems have been tested~ and found to be absolutely , foolproof.

And politicians had reassured them.

Gribble wasn't playing I-spy; he was poking around under his seat. He hoped to find something to play with . . . and he did.
For under the seat he found –

AN UNUSUAL OBJECT

'Gosh,' he thought, 'this antique object looks like it might be one of those horribly powerful, lazy-gun zappy things that Grandad Grott was telling us about.'

I wonder if it still works?

Potato?

Meanwhile, Dimbert was on the train. There was nothing much to see out of the window – just trees and stuff. He consulted the Computer Display Screen to see where he was.
It said:

> We are passing over the arboreal conservation area formerly known as Black...bank Woo....oo!!

Suddenly . . . there was a blinding flash of laser-white light and the sign said:

LAZEPRPR OOh!!
ZARghh!!
Thingy

There was a pause. Then it said:

> Erh........ sorry about that...where was I?..
> ...Oh yes....ALL PASSENGERS ALIGHT HERE..

Dimbert, obedient to the computer's instructions, stepped out of the door.

Had he glanced back at the sign he would have seen that it now said:

> ....Oh... yes......I forgot to mention....Erh..
> PLEASE MIND THE STEP......

But he didn't glance back at the sign. He was too busy hurtling head over heels down into the darkness.

He landed, unharmed, but in a
strange and alien place. Even if he
could have seen where he was he
wouldn't have known where he was.
He'd never been in a wood before.

For a brief moment
the sky was illuminated by
a streak of light, not unlike a
falling shooting star.

Then the spooky darkness
folded around him once more.
And he was scared.
He decided to wait until the street
lamps came on before he made a
move.

                    And so he waited.

But the street lamps didn't come on.

It just got darker.

He was wondering what on earth he could do when . . .
he noticed a flickering light
in the distance.

Civilisation!

he thought,

and started blundering
towards it **but**
he was stopped in his tracks by

a terrible
BLOOD CURDLING
WAIL!!

In the 16th century, minstrels travelled the length and breadth of the land. They sang ditties and ballads, and love songs with words like:

These words probably sounded to you like *a load of meaningless twaddle*. And no wonder; they are 16th-century words.

Things are different now.

We still have minstrels of a sort. And they still go on nationwide tours. We call them pop singers. But how their songs have changed. For their songs reflect the world of fast-moving information technology in which we live. They have words designed to be instantly understood. Words like –

To a 16th-century minstrel these words would sound like *a load of meaningless drivel.*

Odd that isn't it?

This story is set in a future time.

It's 64 years since the Grobblewockians attempted to conquer Earth.

In the course of time the names of things and places often get changed. Especially by people (or aliens) who are doing a spot of conquering.

FOR EXAMPLE :—

You probably know the capital city of England as:

But the place we now call London the Ancient Romans called:

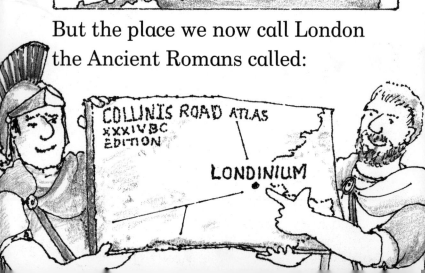

So had Dimbert been walking along the banks of the river Tamesis in 54BC he might have chanced upon a troop of Roman soldiers sitting around a camp fire scoffing oysters and singing:

LONDIN·I·UM'S BRIDGE... ♪ IS NOT YET BUILT ♫ Not yet built... not yet built...

One last example:

STONE AGE CAVE PEOPLE

In prehistoric times most things hadn't been discovered yet. And people then had so few words they probably weren't sure what to call the things they had got.

Can you imagine what Dimbert might have heard if he'd stumbled across some Stone Age Cave men having a sing song?

Back in 1988 Garry Wimbush had told Grott all about Scouting. Grott had then told other Grobblewockians what he'd been told — and they told other aliens what they'd been told. And so the Word spread. But alien memories are unreliable and words get misheard and repeated wrongly.

FOR EXAMPLE:—
Garry told Grott →

A Scout smiles and whistles under all difficulties.

But Grott told the others ↴

A Scout mildly whispers under all difficulties.

By 2052 it was being said that ↴

A Scout likes highland drizzle and adores difficult trees.

This is another way that words get changed... AND EXPLAINS WHY...

Earlier that day, soon after they had landed safely in Blackbank Wood, Grandad Grott had announced:

First of all we must unpick our cat-bugs.

Gribble and the troop unpacked
their kit-bags.

Then they

patched their tonts >

making sure
that their
< tont pigs
were set at 45 degrees,
and knocked in firmly with
[a widden mullet. >

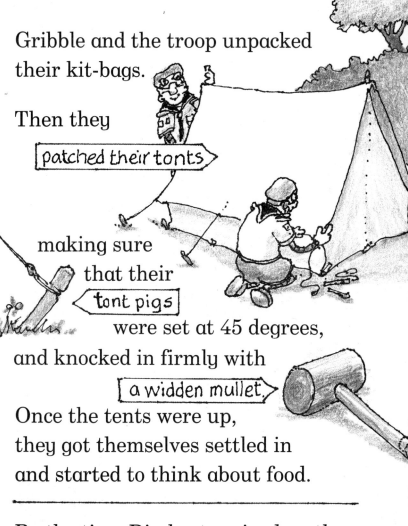

Once the tents were up,
they got themselves settled in
and started to think about food.

By the time Dimbert arrived on the
scene the Grobblewockians had
scoffed a load of sausages, and were
sitting around the 'old camp friar',
having a sing song.

They were singing that old scouting favourite:

Now, not only were these alien Scouts not singing what you would call *the proper words*, they were also not singing what you would call *the proper tune*.

The fact was, they *didn't know* the proper tune. So to conceal this fact they each sang *a different tune* that they *didn't know* . . .

VERY LOUDLY.

It was all too much for Dimbert. He screwed up his face and let out . . . an **almighty howl.**

Which is computer talk for:
"Help! I can't hear myself think!"
The Grobblewockians had been
told that on the planet Erf,
Cub Scouts did . . .

A Grand Howl

. . . but, of course, they'd never
actually heard one. Naturally they
thought that this was what they
were hearing now – and howled
back their reply.

I don't know if you've ever been
unexpectedly grand-howled at
by a troop of alien Scouts,
but if so, you probably said what
Dimbert said next.
He said:

ARgHeeei!!

He then did what anybody in their
right mind would do if an alien
monster wearing Scout uniform
loomed up to them out of the
darkness and said:

Hello there stranger. We are the 3rd Grobblewockians. Would you care for a sossage?

He fainted.

Now, when offered a sausage, the average alien being would usually say something like:

'Oh thank you very much'

– and then eat it.

So when Dimbert screamed:

ARgHeeei!!

– and then lay down on the floor, the Grobblewockians were somewhat confused.

said Gribble. He was always keen to show off his first aid skills.

But Grandad Grott said:

So that's what they did.

49

Next morning the sun rose bright
and early.

NB. When I say "the sun rose early." I don't
mean actually EARLIER THAN IT SHOULD HAVE DONE!
One of the comforting things about
the sun is - it's very punctual. You can
be pretty sure that it will always come
up — dead on time.
But it wouldn't sound very poetic if I said -
"Next morning the sun rose bright and
dead on time," would it? And anyway
it seemed very early to Dimbert...

And it seemed very bright too.
He looked through the tent flap
and, as if for the first time,
saw the outside world.

Edu:/Pixel@*/wwwow:!!
It's like a 3D Graphic from
VIRTUA·LANDSCAPE ; the
multi-media ecology game.

He'd seen the countryside before
but only from a distance. It seemed
different now that he was in the
middle of it.

He was wondering where he was
exactly, and how he'd got there
when he was suddenly reminded.

What do you think he said next?

Now, if **you** were in a strange wood, and were suddenly 'Peep Bo'd' by alien space monsters, would you say: 'Excuse me, I wonder if you'd mind telling me where I am?'

No. You'd be too scared to speak. In fact you'd probably be ***Alienograhorrywobblified!!***

But Dimbert wasn't scared at all. You see, <u>he</u> spent his days playing **'DOOMBATS'** and **'TERRORMAZE'**. And these alien space monsters were not half as ugly as . . .

And they seemed quite harmless too.

'The trees?' enquired Dimbert.
'What about the trees?'

'They don't actually know very
much about trees,' thought Dimbert.
True, he didn't know much about
trees either.
But he did have his MiCROM/P68
InFotek Pocket-size Computer.
He took it out, loaded a programme
entitled

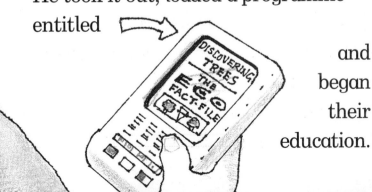

and
began
their
education.

There was something Dimbert didn't understand. If the aliens liked trees, why were they looking so bored?

The reason was simple.

The Grobblewockians knew a few things about trees that Dimbert obviously didn't.

They decided that now was a good time to begin his education. So . . .

They told him about

56

And how a tree could be

A look-out post.

A hiding place.

Or just a comfy place to sit and think.

They taught Dimbert about all sorts of things.
Interesting things, such as . . .

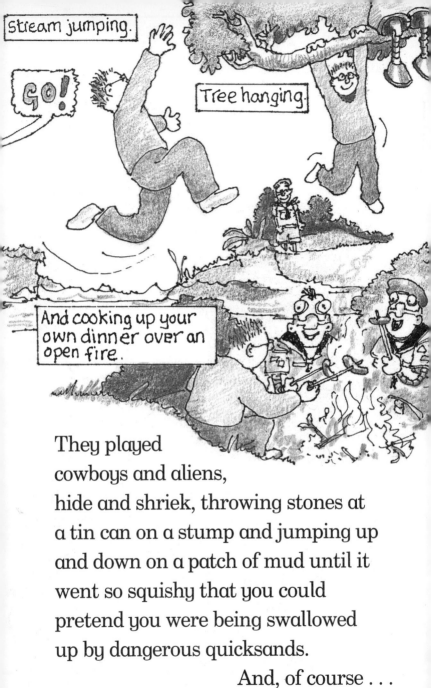

They played
cowboys and aliens,
hide and shriek, throwing stones at
a tin can on a stump and jumping up
and down on a patch of mud until it
went so squishy that you could
pretend you were being swallowed
up by dangerous quicksands.

And, of course . . .

knot naming.

By the end of the afternoon, Dimbert had come to a realisation.

They were sitting
under a horse-chestnut
tree, wondering what
they could do next,
when Gribble
was struck by a good idea.

I know! We could play CLONKERS!

What's Clonkers?

It's a game.

You mean, like LEMMINGS?

60

Grandad Grott had been listening
to the conversation.
'I remember when I first played
clonkers,' he said. 'It was over
fifty years ago, in this very wood.
And d'you know who it was taught
me to play? Our Great Scouting
Leader; Garry Wimbush.
I wonder where he is now?'
'I know where he is!'
                    cried Dimbert.

And they did.

And that's how in the year 2052
Dimbert Wimbush will learn the
meaning of friendship, and discover
the wonders of

THE GREAT OUTDOORS

He will still use his computer to help
him with his homework, of course,
and he'll play games on it too.
But not all the time.
On sunny days and Saturdays,
and on misty, moisty autumn days
he will go out into the real world
of fields and woodland, back streets
and parks, and play games *with
other children*, real games which
they **make up themselves.**
And in the evening, snuggled up
in his bed, tired after a boisterous
day, he will think back with pride to
the day that he took part in . . .

... the first ever ...

THE END